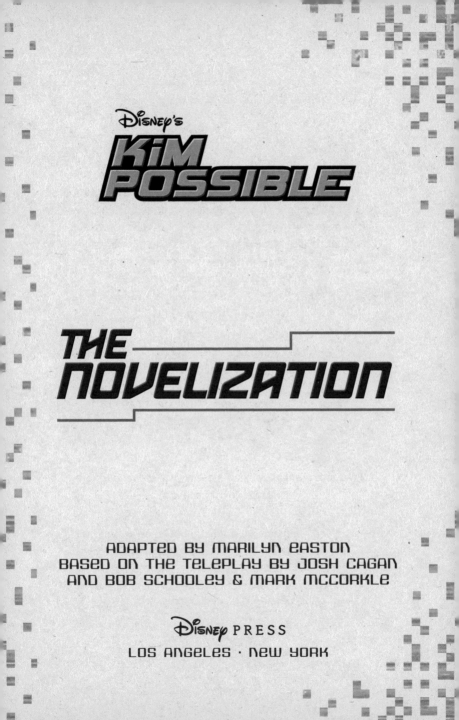

Disney's KIM POSSIBLE

THE NOVELIZATION

ADAPTED BY MARILYN EASTON
BASED ON THE TELEPLAY BY JOSH CAGAN
AND BOB SCHOOLEY & MARK MCCORKLE

Disney PRESS

LOS ANGELES · NEW YORK

Printed in the United States of America
First Paperback Edition, January 2019
3 5 7 9 10 8 6 4 2
Library of Congress Control Number: 2018953271
ISBN 978-1-368-04572-8
FAC-025438-19017

For more Disney Press fun, visit www.disneybooks.com
Visit DisneyChannel.com

SUSTAINABLE
FORESTRY
INITIATIVE

Certified Chain of Custody
Promoting Sustainable Forestry
www.sfiprogram.org
SFI-01054
The SFI label applies to the text stock

So, a few years ago, I accidentally received a distress call.

I was done with my homework, so I answered it.

Now, well . . . I save the world.

Since taking my first call, I've stopped a meteor hurtling toward Earth, rescued a dozen princes, and even wrestled mutant sharks. But no matter the sitch, me and my best friend/best sidekick, Ron Stoppable, face it head-on. And we aren't alone. We've got plenty of help from Wade Load, our tech genius, who sends us vital information whenever we're on a mission. Plus, for every sitch, I've got plenty of cool crime-fighting tech—including a pendant I use to communicate with Wade, called the Kimmunicator.

But my all-time favorite evil-villain-butt-kicking device is my grappling hook. Saving the world involves a shocking amount of grappling hooks.

Every star-student world saver has an archnemesis. Mine is the mad scientist Drakken and his evil sidekick, Shego. Come to think of it, I haven't heard from them in a while. I'll have to check up on them soon. But first, I have a new mission.

Today's sitch: deal with a zillion gallons of world-ending slime. Professor Dementor has kidnapped a big-deal slime scientist and is holding him hostage in his alpine lair.

But it's so not the drama. Because I'm going to rescue him. . . .

Who am I?

I'm Kim Possible.

CHAPTER 1

KIM ACCELERATED HER JETPACK TOWARD A MAJESTIC DAM SURROUNDED BY MOUNTAINS.

As the wind rushed past her, she could see that the structure was holding back a huge reserve of sinister black slime—the handiwork of Professor Dementor. Kim counted double the usual number of henchmen guarding Professor Dementor's lab. Recently, he had suspiciously beefed up his security.

But Kim wasn't worried about the extra henchmen surrounding the lair. She was ready.

Kim silently landed, expertly removing her helmet and letting her red hair cascade down her back.

Inside the alpine lair, henchmen kept watch over a scared-looking doctor bound to a chair in chains. Professor Dementor, dressed in all black with a helmet, walked menacingly down a narrow platform toward the chained-up doctor.

"I've done everything you've asked," the doctor pleaded as Professor Dementor approached him. "I've formulated the world's most dangerous disintegrating slime! Please! Please let me go! I miss my wife, and my kids, and my mold spores!"

Professor Dementor stopped short before him. "My dear Doctor Glopman, you say this is the uber-slime." He motioned to a vat of bubbling purple slime down below the platform.

Doctor Glopman nodded furiously.

Professor Dementor leaned down toward him and said, "Let's make sure."

A henchman spotted Kim outside the lair, alerting the others on his tech device and charging toward her.

She closed the wings of her jetpack and spin-kicked him right in the chest, knocking him down. More henchmen charged at her. Kim stared at them with a wry smile and clicked the button on her sternum, unbuckling her jetpack. She bent over, unfastened the jetpack's harness, and let it rip. It flew straight ahead, knocking down henchmen like bowling pins. Suddenly, two more henchmen closed in on her, each grabbing an arm.

Truth be told, Kim hadn't quite figured out how to get out of this one.

At least not yet.

The henchmen backed Kim up against the dam wall that looked out over a sheer drop to the water below, and she struggled against them. "Yah!" Ron shouted as he fell from the sky and crashed into the two burly henchmen, knocking them over. His helmet flew off. "Are we winning?" asked Ron. He stood up, a dazed look on his face.

"Ron, look at the henchdudes you took out!" said Kim with a proud grin.

"Ron, you've done it again!" he told himself as he removed his jetpack. Just as it slid off his back, the wings popped out and the jetpack flew away, disappearing from view in a stream of smoke.

"I'm *sure* Dementor didn't see that," Ron said, leaning casually against a black barrel full of flammable fluids. It tipped over and hit another barrel, causing a chain reaction that started a small fire.

"Ron, run!" Kim cried out, ducking behind a rusty crate.

Ron dove right beside her just as the fire burst into an enormous explosion.

Ron and Kim stood and examined the damage as the smoke cleared. "Okay, he *might* have seen that," Ron admitted sheepishly.

Kim's pendant emitted a four-note jingle and glowed; then she pressed it and a hologram popped up. The lit-up screen being projected from her Kimmunicator showed Wade, who wore a hoodie and sat in a dark computer-filled room somewhere.

"Kim! I've got a target lock," said Wade. "Here. See for yourself."

The image of Wade's head was replaced with schematics and a map of the building with a big X marked on one of the floors. "Professor Dementor has the scientist chained up on level six," Wade continued. "You better hurry!"

"Let's go, Ron," said Kim, breaking into a run. "We need to stop Dementor before he uses that disintegrating slime!"

Back in the lair, Professor Dementor held a cup of dark slime as he moved past his henchmen. To make sure it was the uberslime, he poured the cup onto a globe. The globe disintegrated immediately. "Success! The world is mine!" he cackled.

Then the slime turned pink and very, very sparkly.

"Why is it turning all pink and sparkly?" Professor Dementor asked.

"I don't know! It's probably just a by-product of the disintegration process!" answered Doctor Glopman from his chair. The panic in his voice was clear.

"I cannot take over the world with the pink and the sparkles! Everybody will make the fun!" shouted Professor Dementor.

"How? They'll all be disintegrated," said the doctor with a sob.

"As will *you*, Doctor Schmarty-Pantses!" shouted Professor Dementor, wheeling on him.

With that, the henchmen grabbed Doctor Glopman and led him to a hook over the vat of slime.

"Now, engage the painfully slow descending hook into your slimy doom!" commanded Professor Dementor.

"Please! Please, don't do this! Be reasonable!" cried Doctor Glopman as the henchmen strung the hook through his chains.

Professor Dementor threw back his head and laughed.

Just then, Kim and Ron busted down a door and descended an eerie staircase that echoed with the sounds of Professor Dementor's cackles coming from somewhere below.

They had to hurry if they were going to save the doctor!

Doctor Glopman dangled over the hissing vat of slime.

Professor Dementor looked on proudly at his handiwork, then adjusted the strap of his helmet.

"Slime's *up*, Professor Dementor!" Kim called

down to him from where she and Ron stood on a platform overlooking the scene.

"Fräulein Possible?" said Professor Dementor incredulously.

Kim gave a sly smile, unafraid.

"Get her!" Professor Dementor commanded, motioning to his huge henchmen, who sprang into action.

"Ron! Unhook the doc, and I'll take the goons," Kim said as she started battling henchmen, delivering one strong move after the next. Henchmen fell around her left and right as she kicked and spun to avoid their attacks.

Kim ducked, jumped, and weaved. Once she tackled the henchmen out of her way, a massive one emerged in front of her, heaving with menace. "Ron, grapple me!" she called out.

Ron tossed Kim her shiny red-and-yellow grappling hook. She triggered it, and it shot out and wound around the henchman! She reeled him in with it, then delivered a powerful kick to his chest that propelled him backward and down. Another henchman charged and grabbed Kim's grappling hook, tossing it into the slime. It completely disintegrated.

"What will you do without your grappling hook, Fräulein!" taunted Professor Dementor.

Kim's eyes narrowed. "Ugh!" she cried out, spinning to kick down the henchman who had doomed her favorite device.

"Oh. That is what she would do," Professor Dementor observed.

Ron struggled to unhook the doctor. The doctor was trying to lift his feet above the slime, but it was dangerously close and getting closer by the second!

"You have to push it and turn," the doctor told Ron. "Push it and turn at the same time!"

"Henchmentors!" Professor Dementor shouted. "Stop that clumsy boy!"

The henchmentors all charged at Ron.

Ron leapt onto the doctor, swinging back and forth over the simmering vat.

"What are you doing back there?" the doctor asked.

"Saving you!" Ron replied.

They both began calling out for Kim.

Kim saw them swinging over the slime and

Professor Dementor below. He was using the remote control to lower the hook. A henchman charged Kim on the platform, and she quickly took him out and pushed him over the railing. The henchman fell and landed on Professor Dementor.

Kim pulled out her lip balm and popped off the top of the tube. A laser shot out. Timing it just right, as Ron and Professor Glopman swung out of range of the vat, she used the laser to cut the chain that held them. They landed safely on the floor beside the vat!

Ron helped the doctor to his feet.

Kim vaulted down the stairs and met them. "Come on, Doc, we gotta get out of here."

"No! I can't!" replied the doctor. "There's a world-ending supply of deadly slime here. We *must* destroy it."

Kim thought for a moment. She glanced at what was left of the slime-covered globe. It wasn't much. Around them, the henchmen were beginning to stir to their senses. She hit her Kimmunicator, and Wade's image reappeared. "Wade! I know we gotta fly, but I need you to see if there's a self-destruct button any—" Ron leaned against the wall. She heard a click. "—where," she finished, turning around to face Ron.

An alarm began to blare, saying something about a self-destruct sequence having been initiated. "Found it," said Ron. He had accidentally hit the self-destruct button.

They had only minutes to escape!

Just then, Professor Dementor pushed the henchman off of him, dashed into a contraption that looked like a coffin with a glass lid, and closed it!

"Looks like I have the only escape pod!" called Professor Dementor from his pod as it readied itself before blastoff.

Kim summoned Wade again. "Hey, Wade, reroute that puppy to the nearest police station," said Kim, her eyes sparkling confidently.

"With pleasure!" Wade responded, hitting a few keys on his keyboard.

Professor Dementor's cackles subsided as he looked down and saw that his escape pod was charted for a new course: the police station. "What? Huh? No! No!" bellowed Professor Dementor. He tapped on the door to the pod, which soon became enveloped in a thick plume of steam. With that, the escape pod launched out of the lair.

Just then, Wade's voice broke through the roar of the escape pod. "Kim! Thirty seconds till self-destruct!"

"Gotta go! Come on!" Kim said to Ron and Doctor Glopman. They raced out of the facility and ended up back on the sunny road overlooking the dam. Kim grabbed her jetpack and strapped it on the doctor. "Take this. Ron and I can share," Kim explained.

"From now on, I will only use my slime for the good of humanity," said the doctor to Kim and Ron.

"And maybe the occasional kids' award show," suggested Ron.

"Drone mode, Wade. Let's get Dr. Glopman to safety," said Kim.

"Can do!" responded Wade.

Kim pressed a button on the jetpack. The doctor rocketed into the air.

"Um, Kim?" Ron said, looking around. "Remember what happened to our only other jetpack?"

The two friends looked down. Ron's jetpack was perched on a ledge far below them, near the bottom of the dam. It was completely out of reach.

The self-destruct countdown hit zero!

Huge balls of fire hurtled toward the black slime lake, turning it into a sparkly pink explosion. The blast headed toward Kim and Ron.

"Okay, I have a plan." Kim grabbed Ron's hand and ran toward the front edge of the dam. The explosion was growing closer. It was a long way down, and neither of them had jetpacks. "Wade! Remote fire Ron's jetpack!" said Kim.

"On it!" replied Wade.

Below, on the ledge, Ron's jetpack fired up.

"Hey, Kim! When I told you that one time I'd jump off a cliff for you, I DIDN'T EXPECT IT TO HAPPEN!" he shouted as she took his hand and sprinted toward the edge of the dam. They both jumped.

Behind them, a flood of slime erupted from the lair and gushed into the air.

Kim and Ron, plummeting, reached out.

Ron's jetpack flew up to meet them. Kim caught it! The evil lair blew sky-high as Kim and Ron sailed through the air to safety.

The mission was complete . . . for now.

CHAPTER 2

IT WAS A BUSTLING MORNING IN THE POSSIBLE HOUSEHOLD.

Kim's parents were going about their day, setting the table for breakfast and watching the morning news as a drone buzzed around the room. The news anchor recited the previous night's news.

"And in Europe last night, teen hero Kim Possible saved the world from a *sticky* situation," the anchor said as an image of Professor Dementor's escape pod in front of a police station filled the screen.

"*Europe?* No wonder Kimmy got in so late," Kim's dad commented as he turned off the television.

Kim's mom ducked as the drone flew overhead.

"I worry about her not getting enough sleep." She added, "Or dissolving into slime." She spotted the drone heading toward her and used a cereal box to push it in a different direction.

"Jim? Tim?" Kim's dad called out to his twin sons just before they bounded into the room.

Equal parts genius and madness, the ten-year-old twins each clutched a remote control that maneuvered the drone. They noticed the drone was going a little haywire.

"Our bad, Mom and Dad!" said Jim apologetically.

"We're still working out some bugs," added Tim.

"Well, I should make sure our gal isn't too tired from her mission to wake up for school," Kim's mom said as she turned to leave.

Meanwhile, Kim was in her room, stretching and getting ready for her first day of high school.

Her backpack was packed, her schedule had been reviewed, and she was just about to wrap up her morning yoga routine.

"Kimmy Ann, the bus is almost here!" her mom called from the doorway.

"Wade?" Kim said from her Warrior One pose. Suddenly, Wade's face appeared on a holographic screen before her.

"The bus will be here in six minutes. You're looking swell today, Dr. P!" Wade said as Kim's mom entered the room. He sipped from a striped soda cup.

"Thank you, Wade. Now, log off. This is a girls-only convo," replied Kim's mom.

"Over and out!" Wade said before he disappeared.

"It's a big day! Do you feel ready?" Kim's mom asked.

Kim stood straight and a huge smile broke over her face. "I'm so excited!" she gushed. "I finished all of my summer reading like two weeks ago. I've done a VR walk-through of the school so I don't get lost. Oh, and my cheer squad audition routine is, if I do say so myself, flawless." She picked up a blue pom-pom and waved it overhead with a bright smile.

Kim's mom clasped her hands together. "Well, I guess that answers my ques—"

"Oh! And look!" Kim, clutching her backpack,

raced across her room and nudged open a panel on the wall. The door opened to reveal racks of new clothes dangling from hooks. Kim tittered gleefully. "I picked out and sorted all of my outfits for the month," Kim said as the rack of outfits pushed out from the wall.

"Wow, for the first month," Kim's mom said, impressed.

"Oh, and I memorized all my teachers' names, their birthdays, their food allergies, just in case we want to get them a gift. And this morning I started prepping for my midterms and finals. Because they are only four and eight months away," Kim explained rapidly. "Can't be too prepared."

Kim's mom, who had been trying to interrupt, took a breath. "Right! Yeah, so you've been really busy since—"

"Three a.m. Well, four a.m. I took a little nap after saving Earth from slimy doom," Kim said with a dazzling smile.

Kim's mom sat down on the bed. She patted the spot next to her.

"Come sit down, my little hummingbird," she said while Kim, backpack on over her cherry-red coat, walked to her.

"What's up?" Kim asked, plopping down beside her.

"My sweet girl," she said, stroking Kim's hair, "I just . . . I want you to know that high school can be kind of daunting. It's okay if you don't figure it all out on the first day."

Kim knew her mom was right, but she also knew she had thoroughly prepared. Everything was crossed off her checklist! "Don't worry," Kim reassured her. "I've allowed myself the morning of day two as well for wiggle room."

"Great," her mom replied.

Kim bolted up. "Mom, don't worry." She put her hands on her hips with pizzazz. "I'm Kim Possible. I handle things. It's who I am. It's what I do."

Kim's mom stood up, smiling. "Sweetie. Just know that we're here for you if you need more . . . wiggle room."

Kim beamed, and they hugged.

Suddenly, Wade's head popped back up in the middle of the room.

"Awwww!" Wade said, recognizing the sweet moment.

"Wade!" said Kim and her mom in unison.

"Sorry! I just got a GPS lock on the school bus. Departure in three minutes," he said in an urgent tone.

"Perfect. Activate the window, please," said Kim, shouldering her bag again. She watched as the huge wall-to-ceiling window automatically slid up behind her. "Okay, Mom. I gotta go. Don't worry. It's just high school. How hard could it be?" With that, Kim somersaulted through her bedroom window, then turned back and waved to her mom. With that, she was off. She couldn't be late for her first day of high school!

Kim had to hurry if she was going to catch the bus. She ran toward the bus stop, pumping her arms as she rounded a corner in the quiet green and sunny suburb.

"Kim, the bus is on your street now!" Wade told her.

As she ran, she saw a woman's baby stroller roll away from her down a hill. Kim sprinted, tumbled, and shot her grappling hook at the stroller, stopping it in its tracks. The cord retracted, pulling the stroller— and the baby inside—back to its owner.

The woman gripped the stroller handle, exclaiming, "Oh, my gosh!" She looked up at Kim and smiled, then tossed her grappling hook back to her. "Thank you, Kim!"

"No problem!" Kim said kindly. With a wave, she was again running toward the bus stop at the end of the street. She could see the bus in view. She was so close!

"The doors are closing!" Wade piped up. He began to count down.

Kim locked eyes with the bus driver, who glowered and began to close the doors to the vehicle.

Kim shot her grappling hook onto a lamppost, which she used to swing herself into the bus just before the folding doors closed. She stood at the front of the bus proudly.

"Made it!" she declared. She looked around. All

she saw was a bunch of completely disinterested kids, most of whom were asleep. And Ron, whose jaw had dropped in awe.

"Booyah!" he cheered.

Kim smiled and quickly took her seat.

CHAPTER 3

DRAKKEN, MAD SCIENTIST AND KIM'S ARCHNEMESIS, WAS IN A GLASS CAGE IN A HIGH-SECURITY PRISON.

He had maniacally decorated his walls with newspaper clippings about Kim's triumphs, which were, of course, his defeats. "Kim Possible, because you foiled my perfect plans all those years ago, I'm stuck in here thanks to you!" Drakken cursed. He looked down. "But I've got you in my grasp now, and there is no escape!" He held a poorly made papier-mâché Kim over the toilet in his cell. "Into the alligator pit with you!" He lowered the doll into the toilet water, shaking it fiercely.

Suddenly, the lights flickered and went out, and he heard what sounded like a punch down the hall. Then he heard a grunt. Then it was silent until . . . *boom!* The door to the room exploded off its hinges. It was covered in a glowing green energy. Shego, Drakken's raven-haired sidekick in a black bodysuit and glowing steel arm cuffs, had come to free him from his prison cell! But Drakken did not look happy to see her.

"Wow. I catch you at a sad time, Drakken?" Shego asked with a laugh and a hand on her hip as she eyed the papier-mâché Kim doll dangling near the toilet.

"Don't sneak up on me like that, Shego! And for your information, this is a scale model revenge simulator," Drakken explained, holding up the doll. In the dim light, the zigzagging blue vein glowed on the side of his face, and his striped shirt looked tattered and worn.

"It's a dolly and a toilet," Shego sharply responded.

"Did you enact my instructions?" Drakken asked, changing the subject.

Shego unwound a roll of toilet paper with lengthy instructions written on it.

"Yes, I followed all the dumb requests you sent me while you were on this enforced vacation. It was *just* as annoying as working with you in person," Shego replied. Her glowing steel cuffs burst into green flames that disintegrated the roll of toilet paper.

"So good to see you, too," Drakken said sarcastically as he began packing items into a pillowcase.

Shego used her steel arm cuffs to blast a hole in the glass cell wall. It was big enough for Drakken to escape through.

"You do know this jailbreak is time sensitive," Shego said snarkily as Drakken continued to pack his things. "Can we move this along? Let's go!" She used her cuff to blast a hole into the ceiling above the glass cell.

"I've been in here for a *year*, Shego! Got a few things to pack, if you don't mind."

"Why do you need all that garbage?" she asked, annoyed.

"For my plan." He stepped out of the hole in the glass cell and took a refreshing breath. "To be the world's greatest evildoer!" Drakken explained.

"And what about Kim Possible? The world's greatest evil-*un*-doer?" Shego asked.

Drakken lifted up his Kim doll. "Possible! Your end is . . . probable!" With that, Shego rolled her eyes. A tractor beam from their hover platform was waiting for them. It pulled them up into the hole in the ceiling, and they zipped away.

Back at Middleton High School, Kim and Ron were stepping off the bus into the bustling crowd of students. Ron lagged behind Kim, recording every moment on his phone. After all, it was their first day of high school. He wanted to make sure to document the momentous occasion.

"Stoppable here, at Middleton High," he reported into his phone.

"Ron, you are *not* live-streaming our first day of school," said Kim, amused by his antics.

"And we are *live*!" Ron said into his phone. "Oh!

This is Kim Possible. We're both a little cranky after saving the world last night."

"I'm so not cranky. I feel great!" Just then, Kim spotted her archrival, Bonnie Rockwaller, through the crowd of students outside the school. Everything stopped for a moment. "Yuck," murmured Kim. Bonnie peered over her giant sunglasses and narrowed her eyes at Kim. Kim narrowed her eyes back.

Kim took a deep breath and tried to smile. It was the first day of school, after all. She wanted to start the year off on the right foot.

"Hi, Bonnie. Did you have a good sum—"

"Kim?" Bonnie asked as she removed her sunglasses. "Kim?" she asked again, as if finally realizing who she was. Bonnie's face broke into a wide smile as she tossed her bag to the nearest girl and approached Kim. "Welcome to high school, my little freshman!" Bonnie, smiling a totally fake smile at Kim, threw her arms around her in an overdramatic hug.

"Hi, Bonnie. Missed you last year," Kim said as Bonnie squeezed her.

"Well, I'm here now. And I want you to think of me as your sophomore big sister!" And with that, she spun on her heel and marched into the high school with Kim's arm linked tightly in hers.

Once they were in the hectic halls, Ron used his phone to document Bonnie. "That's Bonnie. She and Kim have hated each other for longer than they've been alive," he said into his phone.

"Who's he blabbering to? Besides everyone . . . constantly," Bonnie said.

Kim started to explain. "Ron happens to be live-streaming to thousands of devoted fans—"

"Okay, Mom, gotta go. Mom?" He shrugged at Kim. "Huh. I guess she signed off."

Bonnie flashed a faker-than-fake smile and strutted off, jamming Ron's shoulder in the process.

Kim felt the slightest hint of defeat. But then she snapped out of it and called to Bonnie. "Almost forgot, *Bon Bon*, when are cheerleading tryouts?" Kim asked.

"Cheer?" Bonnie said with a snort. She no longer tried to fake being nice. Her expression was deadpan and rude. "You want a *cheer* school? Yeah, go hang with the losers in Lowerton. Here at Middleton High, we're about one thing. This is a soccer town. Tryouts are after school if you're feeling brave." With that, Bonnie whipped a whistle from her pocket. She blew it, and out of nowhere, a soccer ball flew toward Kim, who caught it right before it hit her face.

"You can't use your hands!" Bonnie shouted.

Kim dropped the ball.

Bonnie smirked and said, "Kthanksbye," in a sing-song tone. Long shiny hair flipping, Bonnie turned on her heel again and walked away.

Kim did not look impressed. She took a deep breath, her face flushed. Ron also seemed a little taken aback. Kim's pendant started glowing, and Wade's hologram appeared in front of her. "Kthanksbye!" Wade mocked.

"Make it quick, Wade. We gotta get to home-room," said Kim.

"Remind me to tell you something about that later. Anyway, I don't know if you heard, but Shego sprang Drakken from the joint," Wade explained.

"What?" Kim said, shocked.

"No big, Kim's captured that dude more times

than I've tripped over my own shoela—" Ron said as he tripped over his own shoelaces. Kim caught him before he hit the ground.

"Want me to run a suspicious-activity sweep on all known lairs, Kim?" Wade asked.

"Please and thank you. And what did you want to tell us about homeroom?" Kim asked.

"Oh, yeah, it's on the other side of the school," said Wade.

"No, it's not. I did a VR walk-through," Kim replied.

"No. They renumbered the classrooms over the summer," said Wade matter-of-factly.

"What?" Kim asked, appalled. She was not starting her year off on the right foot. She wasn't even starting it off on the right *leg.*

Just then, the bell rang. She looked at Ron, then at the hallway, and they dashed off, hoping they wouldn't be late on their first day of school.

CHAPTER 4

KIM AND RON BURST THROUGH THE DOOR TO THEIR HOMEROOM, TRYING TO CATCH THEIR BREATH AFTER RUNNING ACROSS THE SCHOOL.

Mr. Barkin, their homeroom teacher, was just wrapping up his morning announcements. He was standing in front of a whiteboard with his name written across it. On the desk next to him, there was a large framed photo of an oversized cat.

"In conclusion, it would be for the best to abandon any hope of joy and find meager satisfaction in monotony." He looked up at Kim and Ron, who were still breathing heavily in the classroom doorway. "Oh! You must be Possible and Stoppable."

"Yeah! He must recognize us from the news!" Ron said with excitement.

"Nope! I recognize you from this," Mr. Barkin said as he held up an attendance sheet, "because you are *late*."

"We got a little turned around. Mr. Barkin, nobody told us they renumbered the classrooms," Kim explained.

"Yeah! I did that. Keeps you kids on your toes," he said. "On your tippity-tippities."

Kim couldn't believe a teacher would do that. "That's not really fair—"

Mr. Barkin picked up the framed picture of a very large cat on his desk. "It takes me ninety minutes to prepare Lady Whiskerboots her low-carb, high-protein breakfast, but that doesn't stop *me* from being on time." He caressed the photo of his cat, then regained his composure. "Anyway, seeing as it's your first day at school, I'm willing to show a little uncharacteristic mercy. But I've got my eyes on both you troublemakers. One each."

"We're not troublemakers!" Kim insisted.

"We're trouble *stoppers*!" added Ron. "Haven't you ever seen us doing good stuff on TV?"

Mr. Barkin gave them a displeased look, his eyes vacant.

Just then the bell rang and all the students filed out past Kim and Ron, pushing them in the process.

Kim tried apologizing to Mr. Barkin once again, but it was no use. She turned to Ron in the hallway. "We gotta get to our first class," she said. Maybe there was still a chance to turn this terrible day around.

"Where is it?" Ron asked.

"Wade," Kim said.

"The other side of the school," answered Wade.

There was no time to panic. Kim had to find a way. "Get me a blueprint of any and all vents, tunnels, and roof access points."

"Comin' at ya!" Wade said as a detailed blueprint of the school popped up in front of Kim.

Kim expanded it with her hand and traced the quickest route on the blueprint. A determined look crossed her face. "Let's roll."

The only way Kim was going to make it to class

on time was to get there in an almost impossible way. Luckily, she was Kim Possible, and she wasn't going to give up. She took out her grappling hook as she ran outside, then swung herself onto the roof. Ahead of her was an air vent.

"Kim! Jump in there!" Wade commanded. She ran across the roof to the air vent and slid through it. Dust and debris flying everywhere, Kim crashed down outside the door to her class. She was out of breath.

Then the bell rang.

Kim stepped inside the classroom and looked up. It was Mr. Barkin and a class full of students already seated attentively at their desks. Again. But how?

"What? How are you here?" Kim asked him.

The teacher closed a textbook he held. "Is your name Kim Possible because it's *im*-possible for you to be on time?" Mr. Barkin asked, upset.

Ron ran up behind Kim. He was also winded, but from running across school the normal way.

"Mr. Barkin?" Ron said, stepping into the classroom.

"Yeah. That's me. I'm subbing for Mrs. Bailey. She's off on eternity leave," explained Mr. Barkin.

"You mean *ma-ternity*?" Kim asked.

"No. I *mean* she's gone and she ain't coming back. Now sit!" Mr. Barkin commanded angrily.

Kim trudged over to her desk.

Her bad day had somehow turned worse. She wished she could disappear. If this was what high school was like, how was she going to survive?

CHAPTER 5

DRAKKEN WANDERED INTO AN ABANDONED, DECREPIT LAIR LOCATED IN A ROTTING SECTION OF THE FOG-COVERED FOREST.

Shego could tell Drakken was not impressed by the cracked stones, outdated evil-science stuff, and overgrown plants that covered every surface. "Gee, thanks for hooking us up with this awesome lab in my absence, Shego," she said, mimicking his voice. "That's you," she told him, for clarity.

"Yes, it's *wonderful* how we used to have our own entire island and now we're squatting in a pile of garbage vaguely shaped like a building!" he replied. He took out his tablet and stuck it in her face. On the screen Shego could see pictures of villains and their secret lairs on a social media site. "I mean, look at Duff Killigan's Villain-stagram! *He* has an underwater base! Señor Senior Senior has an active volcano! We used to have an *island*!"

"Well, that island," explained Shego, marching into the dingy room, "if you remember correctly, slightly exploded."

"Because of Kim Possible!" Drakken hissed.

Shego burst into laughter. "Yeah! Imagine, all your *genius* plans foiled by one puny kid," taunted Shego.

"She isn't just one puny kid. There is something about her that makes her able to defeat villain after villain after villain. A certain . . . spark."

Behind him, Shego fidgeted with her gloves in the shadows.

"And I want that spark," said Drakken. He looked at an old television screen that flared to life with a headline about Kim Possible, and his eyes glinted dangerously.

Back at Middleton High, Kim shuffled down a staircase. "Ugh. What a day. What is high school's deal?"

Ron was walking next to her, trying to make the situation better.

"I gotta tell you, KP, in my fifteen years on this crazy planet, this is the best first day of school I've ever had." They stepped down into the hallway. "Remember sixth grade?" he asked.

Kim thought for a moment. "Today beats losing your pants at the welcome assembly, I'll give you that."

"That's the spirit! And besides, so today was a hot dumpster fire. So what? The Kim I know doesn't go down without a fight! You got this!" Ron said encouragingly.

Kim spun to face him, her eyes lighting up. "You know what? You're so right. I wasn't planning on trying out for soccer today, but how sweet would it be to wipe that smug smile off of Bonnie's face." Kim laughed. "Come on!"

Ron and Kim headed toward the soccer field. They saw Bonnie and the other members of the soccer team on the field practicing as they approached. Kim headed over to them with a smile.

"Okay, Kimber-lumps. It's simple," said Bonnie. Her hair was pulled back into a ponytail, and she and the other girls wore maroon-and-orange soccer uniforms with the letter *M* on the front. "Kick this ball into that goal." She kicked the soccer ball at Kim, who confidently trapped it underfoot. "Oh, and if you don't too terribly mind, my squad and I here will do everything in our power to try and stop you," Bonnie said overly sweetly, tilting her head with a fake smile.

Bonnie's smile fell and she blew her whistle.

Kim wasn't one to back down. She gave Bonnie a smug smile back and arched an eyebrow, up for the challenge.

The girls ran into their positions. From the sidelines, Ron cheered on Kim. "Let's go, KP!" he shouted. The game began. Kim kept her cool, kicking the ball toward the goal. Every step of the way, Bonnie's teammates were there, trying to get the ball away from Kim. But she had something they didn't: she was Kim Possible! Kim jumped, leapt, and even flipped past her opponents—never losing sight of the ball. Kim charged toward the goal with fierce determination. The goalie stood her ground on the right side of the goal. Kim kicked the ball in an epic flip through the air, sending it sailing right past Bonnie—who fell to the ground—and into the goal. It was good!

The soccer team was shocked. Ron whooped and hollered from the sidelines.

Bonnie stood up, blinking. "Okay? From the bottom of my *very* deep heart, Kim, that was . . . amazing. I'm shook," she said sweetly as the team flanked her. "So congratulations to our newest . . . equipment manager." She lightly clapped while two teammates dropped a bin of dirty, stinky clothes and equipment in front of Kim.

"Equipment manager?" Kim asked, unsure whether Bonnie was joking.

"I take just a hint of starch," Bonnie instructed with a smile.

"Equipment manager?" Kim said with a laugh. "Bonnie, you just told me I was amazing!" she protested.

"You totally are, Kiki Peeps. But you're also a freshman," replied Bonnie, turning up her nose and fluttering her lashes in disgust.

"So?" Kim asked, not sure what that had to do with soccer.

"Oh, awkward moment. Did I forget to tell you? So sorry. Freshmen can't be on the team!" Bonnie shrugged with a smirk. "Oh, use a non-chlorine bleach, obvi." Bonnie turned and left with the rest of the team, leaving Kim shocked and also repulsed by the stench from the uniforms.

"Wait, where am I taking this?" Kim asked.

Wade popped up with a school blueprint.

"The equipment room is on—"

Kim eyed the schematics. "The opposite side of the school," she said, unamused.

Kim hung her head for a moment and sighed. Then she took a deep breath—away from the smelly box, of course—picked up the heap of disgusting uniforms, and headed toward the equipment room.

Meanwhile, in Drakken's lair, Drakken and Shego watched Kim haul off the bin of dirty equipment on their television monitor. They had been spying on her.

"So, how's stealing that spark going?" Shego asked Drakken, her voice dripping with sarcasm. She was filing the metal nails of her gloves. "You know," she continued, "besides going poorly."

"Today is her first day of high school," said Drakken. "Something that can reduce the strongest, most confident adolescent to a helpless mewling kitten. This is happening to our little foe as we speak, and once she is at her weakest, I will isolate and steal that spark that makes Kim *possible*!"

Shego rolled her eyes.

Drakken approached a glowing piece of equipment that looked like a vending machine, and pulled its lever down with a cackle. But then the machine beeped, alerting him to a problem, and his smile faded as he inspected it. He turned to Shego. "Um, did you get the Zakadium Q-46?"

Shego looked up. "Huh?"

"It's the power source of my revenge plot?" Drakken said.

"Oh!" Shego pointed to the corner of the room at a stack of grimy cabinets. "Yeah, it's in there," she said.

"Oh." Drakken pulled out a pathetic-looking cardboard box from a compartment and examined it, then looked up at Shego. "You ordered it online?" Drakken asked with disgust.

"Yeah. Get with the times, doc! Nobody leaves the lair anymore," she explained, going back to filing her silver talons.

Drakken opened the box, which was emitting a terrible odor, and sighed. "This is a cheap knockoff!" He dropped the box at Shego's feet. "Get the Zakadium!"

Shego stood up from her chair. "Hey! You know, yelling might make you feel better, but it doesn't make me feel worse. Just an FYI!" she said before storming off.

Drakken took a deep breath. "Just a detour on the road to victory," he murmured wickedly to himself.

Ron had joined Kim's side as she carried the bin of smelly soccer equipment. His attempt at trying to cheer her up wasn't going so well. "You've only been at school *one* day and you're already making a difference! Your arms are going to be jacked by the end of the year, which will be great for when you get on the soccer team and can't use them!"

Kim let out a much-needed laugh. "Thanks, Ron. You know, you always know what to say. Sort of. Regardless, I've had the absolute worst first day of school that any human could have," she said. As they approached a corner, they heard someone crying.

"Or maybe not," said Ron.

Kim set down the bin, and the two friends peeked around the corner and saw a small freshman girl sitting against the wall, sobbing into her phone. She was wearing dull baggy clothes and had a lot of frizzy, unruly hair falling around her face. She was surrounded by books and papers that had been tossed from her backpack.

"It was awful, Mom! I didn't make any friends, and I just tripped and dumped out my backpack everywhere, and . . . everyone laughed." She paused, listening to the person on the other end of the phone. "I know. Love you, too," she said, then hung up.

Kim knew just what to do. With a few perfectly placed cartwheels, Kim picked up all the scattered books and papers. Then she did a backflip, placed everything back in the bag, and handed it to the girl.

"I believe this is yours," she said with a smile. "I'm Kim."

The girl took the backpack. Then her jaw dropped. She was completely starstruck. "I know."

"Are you okay?" Kim asked, growing a little worried when the girl didn't move.

She snapped out of it. "Okay? I just met Kim Possible!" She let out an excited little squeal.

Kim laughed and helped her up. "Come on."

CHAPTER 6

AFTER KIM DROPPED OFF THE UNIFORMS IN THE EQUIPMENT ROOM, KIM, RON, AND THE NEW GIRL HEADED OVER TO BUENO NACHO FOR AN AFTERNOON SNACK.

They settled into a large booth near the window, and Ron left the table to pick up their order. The scent of delicious Mexican cuisine filled the air.

"Bueno Nacho! Love it!" the girl said.

"Yep! It's Ron's 'casa away from casa,'" said Kim with a grin. "I'm sorry! I didn't even ask you what your name was! You didn't go to Middleton Middle School, right?" Kim asked.

"Oh, no. I just moved here this summer," replied the girl. "I'm Athena."

Ron looked over his tray, piled high with paper-wrapped deliciousness, as he approached them. "Ah, Athena, as in the goddess of . . . I want to say *dentistry*?"

"Actually, wisdom," Athena responded. She and Kim laughed.

"If you say so. Well, you've made a *wise* choice today, M'Athena." Ron sidled up next to Kim in the booth and stared down at his tray. "Behold, nature's perfect food, the naco. Taco meets nachos in a fusion of cheesy glory." He picked up food wrapped in paper and waved it at them. "But, of course, you guys ordered—"

"Cha-Cha-Chimirito, no sour cream!" Athena and Kim answered at the same time. They looked at each other and laughed, realizing they ordered the same thing.

"What are the odds?" Athena was trying to play it cool. She couldn't believe she was hanging out with *the* Kim Possible and Ron Stoppable! She tried to sneak a selfie of the three of them.

"Hey, lemme see that phone for a hot sec?" Kim asked.

"Oh! Uhh." Athena handed her the phone shyly. Kim held it up and snapped the best selfie of the three of them. She handed the phone back to Athena. "Seriously, just ask. We're the least selfie-averse people on the planet," she said as Ron nodded in agreement.

"I have followed all of your adventures for, like, *ever.* I cosplayed as you at Comic-Con last year! Look at this!" Athena held out her phone. There was a photo of Athena in a homemade Kim costume, complete with a wig made from a mop painted red. Next to her was a dog dressed as Ron.

"It's . . . amazing," Kim said with a smile. "And that hair!"

"No, it's weak. But I'm working on a better one," replied Athena as she looked away, feeling a little embarrassed.

"What's up with the incredibly handsome pooch?" Ron asked.

"That's Ron Stop-Pit-Bull, of course!" said Athena to Kim and Ron's laughter. "I, uh, didn't really have, uh, friends to go with me. . . ." Athena's voice trailed off.

"I don't know if you know this about me, but when I grow up, I want to *be* a dog. My parents tell me it's not a realistic goal, but thanks to you, I'm one step closer," Ron said.

"Ron, be the dog you want to see in the world," said Athena encouragingly.

"Thank you. And woof."

"Woof, woof, *woof*!" said Athena loudly.

Their whole booth broke out in cheerful laughter.

CHAPTER 7

THE NEXT DAY AT SCHOOL, KIM AND RON WERE LATE—AGAIN.

"The tardy party continues," Mr. Barkin said accusingly.

"I'm so sorry, Mr. Barkin," said Kim.

"Sorry doesn't cut it, young lady! I'm giving you both detention!"

"I can explain, Mr. B!" Athena chimed in behind Kim in the doorway. "We've actually been volunteering at the cat shelter."

"That's no excuse. Wait, I'm sorry, the what?" Mr. Barkin asked.

"Yeah. The cat shelter . . . for all the homeless cats out there. The ones from the streets," Athena said. "They're very protein deficient and have a very low-carb diet."

"So sad," Kim quickly added.

Mr. Barkin's eyes looked misty as he tried not to get choked up. "Well, I suppose I can let it pass. For meow. I mean, now. Now. Sit," Mr. Barkin said.

Kim nodded at Athena and gave her a little high five. If she got in trouble with Mr. Barkin again, she was sure she would get detention. But luckily, Athena had known just what to say.

Later, Athena and Kim were hanging out and listening to music in Kim's bedroom.

Kim had her head buried in a book while Athena touched up her makeup at Kim's vanity mirror.

Athena looked through her bag. "Darn! I left my lip balm at home!"

"Oh, I'm sure I have a spare," said Kim as she touched her Kimmunicator. The panel in the wall slid up, revealing that the wall and vanity were packed with crime-fighting gadgets, disguises, and, of course, grappling hooks.

Athena stared in wonder. "Wow! So many grappling hooks!" she said.

"Saving the world requires a surprising amount of grappling," Kim replied with a chuckle.

Then Athena noticed a familiar outfit hanging on the wall. It was a pair of green cargo pants and a black shirt—Kim's old mission outfit. "Hey! How come you don't wear this on missions anymore? It, like, used to be your thing!" Athena asked.

"Yeah, I don't know," replied Kim. "I guess wearing the same thing all the time kinda felt cartoony after a bit." Kim's fingers traced over her lip balms. "Now, which shade would look the best on you?"

"Oh. Here's one," said Athena, picking up a lip balm.

"Athena, no, that's not—!" Kim shouted as she dove toward Athena, who had opened the lip balm. A laser shot out and made a hole in the wall!

"I am so sorry! I'm such a klutz!" said Athena, panicking.

"No, it's fine!" exclaimed Kim, capping the lip balm and putting it away. "I'm just glad you're okay. Here. This one's safe."

Then an upbeat new pop song started playing

over the speaker. "This song is great! Who is it?" Athena asked.

"It's the new Poppy Blu! It's been all over the Internet for like a month, and I love it."

"Who?" Athena asked.

"Poppy Blu? You've never heard of her?" Kim asked as Athena started dancing goofily. Kim cracked up into a fit of laughter.

Suddenly, Athena felt a little self-conscious. "Oh, my goodness. Are you judging?" she asked.

"No! No, no, no! Of course not. Getting to know you has been—"

"Pretty great," Athena and Kim finished in unison. "Yeah," they said through laughter.

Athena extended her hand to Kim. "Let's dance!"

Kim took it, and they had an all-out dance party.

The next afternoon at school, while the soccer team raced to and fro across the field, Kim sat on the sidelines picking dirt out of old soccer cleats using a toothbrush. Luckily, Athena kept her company, drawing something on a soccer ball with black marker.

Athena turned to Kim. "Hey! You wanna kick this

bad boy around a little? After all, we gotta get ready to make the team next year." Athena tossed the ball to Kim.

Kim caught it. "Can I pretend it's Bonnie?" she asked.

"Way ahead of you," Athena responded as she pointed to the ball. She had already drawn a very realistic portrait of Bonnie's face on the ball.

"It's like you were born to be my BFF," Kim said with a smile.

"I've felt the same thing myself. Let's play," Athena replied.

"Okay," said Kim. "Let's start with the basics. Let's do some juggling." The friends kicked the ball back and forth.

"Oh, wow! Kim, you're so good!" said Athena in awe.

"You try," said Kim, passing her the ball. Athena expertly juggled it with her feet.

"You're incredible!" said Kim. "Pass it to me!"

Athena sent the ball her way, and Kim ran for it. She somersaulted and stopped it under her foot.

"That was awesome!" exclaimed Athena.

They continued playing and trying to show off their coolest moves. Kim did an amazing high-kick move, and then Athena did a slightly better version of it. Athena was learning from Kim and having a great time. Then Kim did an incredible spin-squat-kick move Athena just *had* to learn. Athena replicated it and jumped high.

"You're a fast learner," Kim said encouragingly.

"And you're a great teacher!" said Athena. She looked up and saw Ron jogging over from the other side of the field.

"Athena, dude, you have skills!" said Ron.

"Aw, thanks, Ron," she replied, blushing.

"You know what? How about the next mission that Ron and I go on, you tag along?" suggested Kim.

Athena's jaw dropped. She looked at Ron and he nodded. Then a huge chunk of her hair flew into her mouth. "Okay, I'm gonna freak out about this eventually, but first I'm gonna go home and shave my head," Athena said.

"I think I have a better idea," said Kim.

Kim, Ron, and Athena arrived at the Salon De S'Lauren.

The elegant entrance had classy floral arrangements and a beautiful fountain. The air smelled crisp, with a hint of vanilla and jasmine. Kim and Ron had to basically push Athena to get her through the frosted glass doors.

"This place is way too nice! Can't we just go to Mega-Cuts? They give you a lollipop!" Athena said as she looked around wide-eyed at the fancy mirrors and luxurious seats.

"And if you're good, they let you sit in a chair that looks like a race car!" added Ron.

"Okay, fam, settle down," said Kim.

"But what do I even tell them to do?" Athena asked from her seat.

Kim placed her hands on Athena's shoulders. "First, breathe. Second, close your eyes. Picture the best version of yourself. You see her?" Kim asked.

Athena opened her eyes. She looked directly at Kim. "I do," she answered.

"Boom! That's the person I want you to be. I

can't wait to meet her!" Kim smiled and gave Athena a hug.

"Me too," said Athena quietly.

Ron and Kim headed over to Bueno Nacho for a snack while Athena got her hair styled. They settled into their usual booth and started eating. Then Kim's pendant started glowing. She tapped it, and Wade's head popped up. "What's the sitch?" Kim asked.

"Shego just blasted into a top-secret government lab," he said urgently. "I'm sending someone to pick you guys up now."

"Tell your recruit it's mission time. Ron, suit up," Kim said as she darted away.

"Just one more bite," Ron said, shoving a naco in his mouth. Suddenly, Kim reappeared, suited up in her mission outfit. "Are you ever going to tell me how to do that?" Ron asked.

"Do what?" Kim asked innocently. She smiled. "Come on, let's go!"

First they headed to the salon to grab Athena. Just as they approached, Athena was walking out the door wearing a new purple-and-black mission outfit. Her haircut, with its red highlights, looked amazing. But it also looked exactly like Kim's.

"Whoa, Athena! You look amazing! You've out-Kimmed Kim! Where'd you get that?" Ron asked.

"Okay, well, don't laugh, but remember when I said I was working on a better Kim cosplay? I actually decided to make myself a mission suit, in case a time came I had to battle evil, and today is that day!" Athena said, looking at Kim's mission outfit.

"It's . . . perfect," said Kim.

Athena smiled. "Oh my gosh, thank you! And with the hair, it's—"

"It's *extra* you," Ron said to Kim.

Suddenly, a pink stretch limo pulled up in front of the salon. "That's our ride!" said Kim. The door opened, dance music blasting from inside the limo. A supercool pop star stepped out in fierce silver heels, a shiny blue jacket and hat, sunglasses, and hoop earrings. "What's the sitch?" It was Poppy Blu! She high-fived Kim and pulled her in for a hug.

"Good to see you, girl!" said Poppy Blu.

"You too, thanks for the lif—"

"Poppy Blu! Oh my gosh! Poppy Blu! I've been a

fan of your music forever!" Athena said, barely able to control her excitement. Kim was confused. The day before, Athena hadn't even known who Poppy Blu was.

Poppy glanced at Athena. "Oh my gosh! Your hair is on point! Who are you?"

"I'm Athena, the newest member of Team Possible!" Athena replied.

"Kim, you're going to have to watch out for this one. Because she is fierce! And I should know because, you know, I invented fierce," Poppy said, singing the last word.

"That was amazing! Okay, so how do you know Kim? Did she save you from someone, like zombies? Ninjas? Zombie ninjas?" Athena asked rapidly.

Poppy sighed. "Worse, the IRS. It turns out Kimmy here is a wiz with international tax law. Anyway, this train is leaving the station! All aboard!" she said, singing the last note so that Athena could sing it in harmony with her. As the two girls sang, Ron and Kim ducked into the limo.

"You are so awesome!" Poppy told Athena. "I like you! You want to come on tour with me?"

Kim glanced at Ron. She felt a little off-balance. First Athena copied her hairstyle, and now she was stealing her friend? Maybe she needed to take Poppy's advice and keep a close eye on Athena.

"Guys, come on. We gotta find Shego," Kim said from inside the limo.

CHAPTER 8

POPPY DROPPED OFF KIM, RON, AND ATHENA NEXT TO A MOODY, SOGGY BOG THAT LOOKED NOTHING LIKE A SECRET GOVERNMENT LAB.

As the limo pulled away, Ron said, "A secret island. Classic."

"Wade, any intel on the secret entrance?" asked Kim.

"I'm working on it, Kim. This one is more secret than usual," replied Wade.

The group walked past a tree with a single apple hanging from a low branch. Athena tugged on the apple. It was attached to a steel cable. Something started rumbling underground. Suddenly, the grassy ground opened and a platform appeared before Kim.

"Wow! Athena, how'd you figure that out?" Ron asked, clearly impressed.

"I don't know. That is not an apple tree," Athena explained with a shrug. "Kim?" Athena asked, looking for reassurance in her skills.

"Solid sleuthing there, buddy," answered Kim with a pat on Athena's shoulder. They all stepped onto the platform and it lowered them down into a very shiny modern underground lab. Flashing emergency lights and broken equipment lay scattered around the room. There was green smoke coming from multiple smoldering areas, and a giant hologram of a brain.

"What *is* this place?" asked Ron.

"'The Institute for Advanced Neurodynamic Studies,'" Kim read off a sign hanging on the wall.

"I've heard of this place. They're making amazing breakthroughs uploading exabytes of data directly into the human brain," Athena explained.

Ron stood in front of the giant fake brain. "Wow! I had no idea brains were that big. How do they fit in our heads?" he wondered aloud.

"Focus, Ron," Kim and Athena said in unison.

Athena looked at Kim with a smile. Kim smiled back. They all traveled down a pair of abandoned stairs, Kim's flashlight shining through the dark at the empty lab.

Various schematics were lit up on glass screens. There was no one there.

Kim tapped her pendant. "Hey, Wade, it's spooky quiet in here. Did we miss her?"

"Shego might be using a cloaking device. She's in there, but I can't pick up heat signatures," he replied.

Athena pushed in front of Kim to talk to Wade. "Did you try running a 6880 Thermal Security Override?"

Wade looked impressed. "I didn't! Good call! I'll give it a try—"

"Never mind! We got it," Kim interjected.

Ron was wandering alone around empty habitat tanks when he noticed a big glass tank half filled with dirt. A sign next to it read NAKED MOLE RAT HABITAT.

"Naked mole rat. Naked. Ha!" Just as he turned to continue looking around, Ron noticed a slight movement on the surface of the dirt. "Hello? Anyone home? You decent?" he asked.

Just then, a tiny, hairless mole rat with buckteeth poked its head out of a hole. It looked scared and alone.

"Oh, wow! Coolest thing ever!" Ron shouted, frightening the mole rat. It instantly went back in the hole. "Sorry! Didn't mean to scare you, little guy. You can come out now. You're safe with me." The mole rat peeked its ugly-cute head out again. "Aw, you're shy. And weird. And I like weird! Never be normal, that's what I always say." He picked up the naked mole rat and then took off, racing to catch back up with Kim and Athena, who still couldn't find signs of Shego anywhere.

"Ron? Did you find anything?" asked Kim.

"I sure did! Kim Possible, meet Rufus Stoppable," he said, holding up the naked mole rat for Kim to see.

Kim was confused and slightly grossed out. "Hey, little guy." She looked to Ron. "What is he?"

"Naked mole rat. Yeah," answered Ron.

"I wonder what they were going to do with you, little guy," Kim wondered aloud.

"Hey! I bet they were testing the brain data

transfer process on these little guys before trying it on humans!" Athena leaned toward Rufus. "Hey, buddy, am I right? Did they make you supersmart?"

"Oh man, Drakken is going to unleash an army of supersmart mole rats!" Ron said, considering the idea. "Better hide in my backpack, buddy." Ron tucked Rufus safely into his backpack.

"Or maybe Drakken wants to be able to download vast amounts of information into his *own* brain. But to do that, he would need some kind of modulator that translates machine learning into brain waves. Kim? Can I talk to Wade again?" Athena said rapidly.

Kim wasn't so sure. "I—"

Athena clicked Kim's pendant. "Wade! Can you run a check on the lab for any sort of Zakadium-based brain modulators? M-21? T-43?" Athena asked.

"Q-46!" Wade responded.

"Bingo! Where is it?" Athena asked excitedly.

Wade consulted a blueprint of the lab. "Sector twelve! To your left!"

"And that's where we'll find Shego! Come on!" Athena said as she ran off with Ron.

Kim didn't join them. She felt left out. "I was just about to say we need to find the brain modulator power cube thing," she said quietly to Wade.

"Really?" asked Wade.

Kim sighed, minimized Wade from view, and ran after her friends. Why wasn't she on her A game?

CHAPTER 9

SECTOR TWELVE WAS FULL OF EQUIPMENT AND EVEN MORE ANIMAL CONTAINMENT TANKS.

Shego was on top of a tall tower of machinery in the center of the room, reaching for a glowing, levitating blue cube.

Kim, Ron, and Athena saw her just as she snatched it.

"Shego!" Kim shouted.

"Possible! It's been too long," Shego responded.

"Can't say I was feeling particularly nostalgic," said Kim.

"Hey, step away from the cube and put your

hands where I can see them!" Athena commanded, stepping in front of Kim.

Shego looked down at Athena. "Who's this?" she asked.

"She's with me," Kim explained, stepping in front of Athena.

"Yeah, why is *she* the one giving me orders, though? Oh! Is she in charge now? Did you get *demoted*?" Shego asked tauntingly.

"Enough talk, Shego." With that, Kim launched into motion as she and her friends split up. Shego used her steel arm cuffs to send green laser blasts down at them, and they dodged right and left.

Shego dove down from the tower and landed on the ground beside Kim.

Kim kicked at Shego, blocking and defending herself from Shego's blows. Finally, Kim knocked the glowing cube out of her hand, and it skittered across the floor toward Athena. "Athena, the cube!" Kim called. But just as Athena grabbed it, Shego shot a blast at it, causing the cube to launch higher into the air. It landed back on the tower platform far above.

"Ugh! I just got that thing down!" Shego said with annoyance.

Shego and Kim raced up the tower of machinery toward the blue power cube. Kim grappled there first, grabbing the cube. Shego leapt sky-high and was struggling with her, trying to get the cube, when a laser blast flew past her head.

As Shego fell and dangled from the edge of the tower, Kim looked down at the source of the blast. It was Athena. She was holding the lip balm laser. "What are you doing?" Kim shouted.

"Sorry! I was just trying to help. I borrowed it from your room. I didn't think you'd mind, considering—" answered Athena.

"It's okay! I got this!" Kim said firmly, not seeing Shego dig her metal claws into the glass of the platform to climb back up.

"No, you don't!" said Shego. She took Kim's momentary distraction as a chance to kick her off her perch. Kim and the cube went flying. Midair, Kim shot her grappling hook into the ceiling and saved herself from falling to her doom. She swung straight for the cube, but Ron was going for it, too.

"I got it!" they both called as they crashed into each other.

Meanwhile, the cube landed on the ground, and Athena bolted for it. The collision caused Kim and Ron to fly into a glass containment tank that was filled knee-high with murky water. The container shook with the force of their landing, causing the hatch on top to close with a click. Ron and Kim were trapped inside!

"Ron! Are you okay?" Kim said through heavy breaths.

"This water is like the perfect temperature," Ron responded in a relaxed tone. "Not too hot, not too cold—" Just then, something slithered by him in the water.

"Ron. Ron! Ron! Get up! Get up!" Kim shouted. "There's something in the water with us!"

While Kim and Ron tried to figure out what creature was trapped with them inside the habitat, Athena had reached the cube, grabbing it just as Shego approached her.

"You're next, new meat," Shego threatened.

"Uh, guys? Little help?" Athena said with a quiver in her voice, backing away from Shego.

Kim pushed on the glass wall of the habitat. It didn't crack. It was sturdy!

Shego had Athena backed up against a wall. "I'm afraid your little besties can't come out to play right now. It's just me and what's about to be left of you."

Athena whimpered.

Just then, the water in the tank started to glow. Kim and Ron felt a zap.

"Fight the fear, KP. They're fascinating creatures! Did you know electric eels can spawn thousands of babies at any given time?" Ron looked at Kim. That piece of information was not helpful.

"What?!" Kim screamed. She turned and banged against the glass. "Athena, help!"

But Shego had Athena cornered. Shego blasted at Athena, who hit the floor and released the glowing blue cube. It slid across the ground and stopped at Shego's feet. She picked it up victoriously. It wasn't looking good for Athena, but then she spotted a long plastic stick with a loop at the end by her feet. She picked it up, standing, and used it like a bo staff to combat Shego. The villain was clearly impressed.

Shego turned to the habitat containing Kim and Ron. "I know you're busy right now, Kimmy, but you've got some competition here! This one's good! Maybe even better than you!" Shego taunted.

Athena launched the long plastic stick at Shego, who dove out of the way. But Athena didn't stop there. She twirled the stick expertly, delivering hit after hit to Shego. Finally, she twirled through the air and smacked Shego so that she flew across the room and hit the wall, dropping the cube in the process.

"Athena! Athena! Help!" Kim screamed as the electric eel in the tank was about to strike.

Athena had to choose. On one side of the room, Ron and Kim were about to be eel-zapped. On the other side, Shego was stirring from the floor. The cube sat between them. Athena made her decision. She ran over to the tank, knocked the lock off with her staff, and released her friends. Ron inspected Rufus for any harm. He was perfectly intact. And still very naked.

The friends could hear sirens and helicopters outside. Shego stood triumphantly on the tower platform, the cube in her gloved hand and a grin on her face.

"Well, this has been a kick. Next time we meet I'm going to have to up my game to match *new meat* here. You know, because she's a *real* opponent, Kim," Shego said. She blasted a hole in the ceiling. A tractor beam appeared and lifted her up to the hover platform's ladder. Shego had escaped. Kim, Ron, and Athena could hear cops outside shouting, "She's getting away!"

"Athena, I knew you had good moves, but your fight skills are sick!" Ron said to Athena.

"Thanks! I'm just a Kimitation. I've studied *all* her moves," explained Athena.

Kim stared up at the hole in the ceiling that Shego had escaped through. She had really dropped the ball, or rather, the cube. Shego's words echoed in Kim's mind. *This one's good! Maybe even better than you . . . better than you . . .*

After her clash with Athena, Shego was soon reunited with Drakken.

She walked into the dingy secret lair as he played back footage of Kim and Ron trapped in the tank on his screen. It gave him great joy to watch Kim struggle.

"Hate-watching your favorite show again?" Shego asked.

Drakken bolted up and walked over to Shego. "You got the Zakadium! Sweet!"

Shego lobbed the cube to him, and he caught it, nearly fumbling it.

"Careful!" he shouted.

"Don't worry, that thing got dropped like six hundred times. It's fine. Anyway, as much as I hate to admit it, you were right. Possible is like your hairline. She's fading," Shego said.

Drakken sighed, running his hand over his head. "Well, you think she's bad now, wait until this clip of her being terrified out of her wits gets 'accidentally' leaked online. Imagine the memes!"

Possible . . . your end is highly *probable,* he thought with an evil grin.

CHAPTER 10

THE NEXT MORNING AT SCHOOL, KIM NOTICED A GROUP OF STUDENTS HUDDLED AROUND A PHONE, WATCHING A VIDEO.

They each had a sticklike object in their hands. It was weird.

"This throw-down is sick!" said one student.

That was when Kim noticed that the sticks the students were holding were all shaped like bo staffs. They were attempting to reenact Athena's signature pole-vault spin-kick move. Poorly.

"Athena is absolutely *destroying* Shego."

"And that hair! Can you believe she goes to our school?"

They all laughed. Kim felt her stomach clench.

At lunch, Kim and Ron watched more students trying to copy Athena's fight moves.

Mr. Barkin's voice came over the loudspeaker. "A reminder, students, no stick, dowel, or rod play on school property. No matter how utterly effortless Athena made it look in the video I have watched nine times."

Kim sank farther into the bench at the table. Ron took out Rufus to introduce him to cafeteria food. Rufus crinkled his nose in disgust. He retreated back into Ron's backpack.

"Rufus," said Kim.

"He's having a hard time adjusting to the high school social whirl." Kim gave Ron a look. He realized what he'd just said. Just then, a voice cut through the air, and Kim looked over to see who it was.

Bonnie said, "You're the best!" to Athena, who was walking next to her. "Your moves are great. Your style is flawless. I mean, that hair! Perfect lip shade, perfect outfit, and those boots! Tens across the board!"

"Aw, Bonnie, you are seriously so nice," said

Athena with a smile. She spotted Kim and Ron. "Hey, guys!" She lowered her tray onto the table next to Kim.

Bonnie turned back and smiled at Athena. "See you after school!"

"After school?" Kim asked, looking up from her lunch.

"Oh, yeah, Bonnie really wants me to try out for soccer," Athena explained. "Which is weird because I know they don't take freshmen, but she just laughed and said not to worry."

Kim felt a little queasy. How come things seemed so easy for Athena?

The rest of the day passed by in a blur. During soccer practice, Kim picked dirt out of the girls' cleats from the sidelines. She watched Bonnie welcoming Athena to the team, handing Athena her new soccer uniform. The whole team practically cheered Athena's name as they tossed dirty towels at Kim in passing. The soiled towels hit Kim in the face. She just blinked and scrunched up her face, like she was stuck in a bad dream.

Later, Kim strolled into Bueno Nacho to find Ron

and Athena laughing together in a booth. That was Kim and Ron's booth. Kim turned on her heel and headed straight back out.

To make matters even worse, Kim got a copy of the *Middleton High School Journal* and saw the headline. Athena was named Student of the Month.

Kim sighed. She felt . . . off.

Kim knew there was only one person who could make her feel better.

Later that day, she knocked on the door of a quaint, cozy-looking home, and the door flew open.

"Kimberly Ann!" It was Kim's grandmother, Nana Possible. She looked just like Kim, except she was a much older version. She had glasses and shoulder-length red hair with bangs and wore a floral pink apron over a red blouse. She beamed at her grand-daughter.

"Hey, Nana," said Kim.

Nana let Kim into the house and picked up a plate of brownies. "Lucky for you, I made a batch of brownies this morning. Double chocolate chocolate chip with pecans on top," Nana said with a twinkle in her eye as they sat down in the library.

"No thanks. I'm good," said Kim rather glumly.

"You're turning down *double chocolate*?" Nana asked in shock. Her look turned sweet as she removed her glasses and smiled. "Feel up for a—"

"Workout?" Kim interjected, returning the smile.

Nana nodded. She reached over to her doily-covered piano and played a few notes. Suddenly, across the room, a shelf of books and knickknacks parted to reveal a hidden training room!

Kim and Nana entered the secret room, and Kim started to stretch, preparing for her workout. "So, Nana, I was hoping today you could teach me to fight with a bo staff."

Nana tossed her a long stick and expertly twirled her own.

"Bōjutsu began in the early seventeenth century in Japan." Nana swung her bo staff at Kim as they began to spar. "But it seems to me, not much call for a bo staff today. Bit of an antique. And it takes one to know one," Nana said with a wink. She swung her staff again, locking it against Kim's.

"It's just that I, uh . . ." Kim started.

Nana could tell something was up. "I did see on the Internet, that new girl . . . She used a bo, didn't she?" asked Nana.

"Yeah, she kicked Shego's butt," said Kim, continuing to spar with her nana.

"You've done that plenty of times yourself. Without a bo," Nana reminded her, pointing her staff at Kim.

"I thought I'd try something new," Kim said, trying to sound convincing.

"Nothing wrong with that. If that's the reason," said Nana.

They continued to spar until Nana landed a hit that caused Kim to tumble to the ground.

"Something's off," said Nana.

"Ugh! Me! I'm off!" Kim said from the floor.

Nana helped her up. "Why?" Nana asked with concern.

"Because I walked into high school and it's like I stopped being good at things. Even worse, Athena had one good fight, and now she's amazing at everything!" Kim explained, sitting on a set of stairs.

"She's your friend, right?" asked Nana.

"Yeah . . ." Kim responded.

"Well then, you should be happy for her! After all, you guided her. Now she's having a little success, all thanks to you," Nana said. She paused and sat beside Kim. "What is it, baby?"

"I've never met someone who's better than me, and I know how stupid that sounds, but it's like, whatever I have that makes me . . . me, she has more of it!" Kim felt her eyes fill with tears. "If I'm not the best at those things . . . then who am I?" Kim said, realizing what was truly bothering her.

"That's just the thing. Even if you're not the *best* at *what-have-you*, you're still you," Nana said in a comforting tone.

"Nana, I'm Kim Possible! I'm a star student and I save the world! That's who I am—"

"No, no," Nana interrupted, holding out a finger. "That's what you *do*. That's not who you *are*."

Kim folded her arms. "Well, then, I . . . don't know who I am," said Kim as her thoughts trailed off. Her mouth quivered. Sobbing, Kim took off.

CHAPTER 11

THE NEXT DAY, ONCE KIM ARRIVED AT SCHOOL, THINGS STARTED OFF ON A ROUGH FOOT.

"Attention, students!" blared the morning announcements on the school intercom. "During last period today, we will holding an all-school assembly. We will honor our star student, Athena, with the first-ever Most Promising Freshman of the Year award!"

Kim froze. She couldn't believe it. It was like the universe was mocking her. She sat down at the back of her classroom and pulled out her phone. She saw pictures of herself on Villain-stagram, with the caption *Washed-up heroes: where are they now?* Then her teacher plucked her phone from her hand and dropped her trig paper on her desk. It was marked with a big red F.

Kim had had enough. She stood up and marched to the nearest exit.

"Kim! School's not over yet!" Ron called, running to catch up to her.

Kim turned to Ron. "I'm ditching. I can't even get good grades anymore. Everything's changed."

Ron stood in front of Kim. "Look! I'm not gonna lie. It's been a rough few weeks. But you're still my best friend. And pals support pals, always," said Ron.

"I think I know where you're going with this," Kim said, staring at her best friend and cracking a smile.

"Athena's our pal, too. We helped her when she was down in the dumps. And our help paid off! She's amazing now. So we should be there to cheer her on," Ron continued.

"So, we're going to this assembly?" said Kim.

"Yeah, we owe it to her," Ron said.

"Ugh. Fine," Kim said, knowing he was right.

"Booyah!" Ron cheered as they headed toward the assembly.

The high school auditorium was jam-packed. Kim and Ron found seats up in a balcony in the back. On the stage, Athena sat next to Mr. Barkin, who was standing behind a podium. He was wearing a blazer with a cat sweater underneath. A banner that hung above them read MOST PROMISING FRESHMAN.

"All right. Attention, students. Settle! In the short time that she's been at this high school, she's earned a five-point-five GPA, is a rising star on the soccer team, and has already been voted home-coming queen *and* king!" Mr. Barkin announced. The crowd erupted in applause. Kim mustered up a few claps.

"It is my great pleasure to introduce your most promising freshman of the year, Athena!" Mr. Barkin cheered as she stood and shook his hand.

"Why is an ominous green circle being cut in the ceiling?" Ron asked, pointing. Kim looked up as a hole appeared in the auditorium ceiling. The ceiling collapsed inward. Debris landed on the floor, and all the students scattered, running away. Shego beamed down onto the floor.

"Everyone, remain calm and walk to the exits in an orderly fashion," said Mr. Barkin.

Shego sent a blast his way, and he ducked. It hit a column of balloons on the stage.

"And I'm out," said Mr. Barkin, fleeing.

Drakken beamed down and addressed the frightened audience. "Good afternoon, students. Don't be alarmed. We're only here to kidnap Athena—"

"Ron, grapple me!" Kim shouted.

Ron handed Kim her grappling hook.

"—before she becomes so powerful, she wipes out evil as we know it!" finished Drakken.

Kim aimed her grappling hook.

Shego aimed her steel arm cuff at Athena. "Let's go," she ordered.

"What? No! Kim! Help!" Athena cried out.

Kim sprang into action, swinging on her grappling hook to the auditorium ground below. She delivered a swift kick to Shego, knocking her over and misdirecting the fiery green blast so that it hit the banner above Athena.

"Henchmen! Attack!" commanded Drakken.

"Hench*women,* attack!" called Shego as a group of henchwomen in all black invaded the auditorium.

Drakken was confused. "Henchwomen? Really?"

"Yeah, dude. It's a new era. Lean in," Shego replied as she ran after Athena.

Kim was being bombarded by henchwomen. She tried to fight them off, but her grappling hook clattered to the floor. She tried to call Wade. But she wasn't wearing her Kimmunicator!

"Ladies! Please escort Cinderella to her pumpkin!" Shego called to her henchwomen. They surrounded Athena.

Kim spotted a mop out of the corner of her eye.

"Kim! Help! Throw it to me! I can do my killer move!" Athena called.

Kim went to toss Athena the staff, but then she hesitated.

"Throw it, Kim!" Ron called from the audience.

"Come on!" cried Athena.

Kim felt determined. She grabbed the stick and ran, attempting to do Athena's pole-vault spin kick. But the stick caught on the floor! Kim tumbled and landed in a heap. It was an epic fail. The crowd gasped.

"Oh! Faceplant!" Drakken cackled.

Shego laughed. "Please tell me someone got that fail on video." She looked out into the audience. Half the students were holding up cell phones, clearly recording the action. Then Shego grabbed Athena and they lifted off into the tractor beam with Drakken.

Drakken cackled. "I'm sure you're wondering what's next!" he called from above. "Well, it's my most diabolical plan yet—"

"Shut it! What have I told you about overshare?" Shego said firmly.

"Oh, right. Welp! Bye!" Drakken said. And with that, he and Shego beamed up into the hovercraft and zipped away with Athena trapped inside. Kim scrambled to her feet and raced outside.

But it was too late. Drakken's hovercraft zipped through the sky and out of view.

Mr. Barkin had followed Kim outside. "Possible, I was up all night making that banner," he said, and stormed away, leaving Kim alone with Ron.

Kim felt completely shattered. "I blew it, Ron. This was my fault," she said sadly, sitting on a bench.

"Oh, come on. It's . . . well . . . yeah. It's your fault," he said, taking a seat beside her.

Kim paused for a moment. She reviewed the events of the past few minutes in her mind. "What was I thinking? I should've just given her the bo staff," said Kim.

"Why *didn't* you give Athena the bo staff?" Ron asked in return.

"Because I . . . I needed to be the person who saves the day," she answered.

"How'd that go?" Ron asked.

"Real, real not great. Very bad," replied Kim.

"How do you feel?" Ron asked.

"I just . . . I can't believe how mixed-up I've been. Like, just because I'm not the best at something doesn't mean I'm not *me*," Kim said.

Ron looked at Kim. "So, what are we gonna do?" he asked with a smile.

Kim's eyes narrowed and she stood up confidently. "We're gonna go save our friend. You up for this? Let's go." She took Ron's hand and they raced off.

CHAPTER 12

DRAKKEN DRANK FROM A CARTON OF COLD SKIM MILK IN HIS LAIR. Shego was sitting off to the side, flipping through a magazine. She was quite bored.

"Shego! Come and celebrate with me with an ice-cold milk!" said Drakken.

"Never let it be said you don't know how to party, Doctor D," said Shego unenthusiastically.

Drakken grinned. "I have to admit, today went better than I could have hoped," he said.

"Yeah. I'm always good. But I felt particularly fierce," said Shego.

"Oh, come on. You were your usual competent self, but I was the *most*," Drakken said.

"*Pft!* The *most average,* maybe!" Shego said tauntingly.

"Will you two stop arguing?" Athena shouted.

"Excuse me?" Shego asked, turning to Athena, who had been watching them from a chair.

"I was just trying to get your attention. And a little credit!" She stood up. "After all, *I* befriended Kim. *I* surpassed her in every single way, and *I* broke her. Just like you asked me to. It was me! I did all of it," said Athena proudly.

"She gets this from you," Drakken said to Shego.

"Don't make me hurt you," Shego replied sharply to Drakken. "So *what*?" she said to Athena. "What do you want? A gold star? A cookie? You want a hug?"

"No, I want to know what's next for the three of us," Athena responded.

Drakken and Shego glanced at each other.

"Huh. Well. It's a . . . surprise," explained Shego with a hint of menace.

"Yes. And you're going to find out *very* soon," added Drakken.

Drakken and Shego shared a good laugh. Athena smiled. She was a little confused.

Back at Kim's house, Ron and Kim were suited up for their mission. Kim's nana, dad, mom, and twin brothers were in the living room, playing with the drone.

When Kim's mom saw them, she bolted up from the couch to greet them. "Kimberly Ann!"

"Hey, sweetie," Nana said to Kim.

"We heard about Athena. We're really sorry," added Kim's mom.

"Oh. It was my fault," Kim explained.

"Yeah, we heard about that, too," said Nana.

"So, I'm going to try and fix that mistake. I don't know if I can. But I think I'll have a lot better chance if I get some help. So, Mom? Nana? Are you in?" Kim asked.

Kim's mom and nana looked at each other. Kim and Ron watched them hopefully.

Nana put her hands on her hips. "Well, you can count on me. I don't know about your mom."

Kim grinned.

"Of course she can count on me!" said Kim's mom. "She can always count on me."

Kim's mom and nana vanished around the corner and reappeared in their slick mission outfits.

"You guys, too? How do you do that?" Ron asked with pure wonder about their lightning-quick outfit changes.

"Do what?" the Possible women answered innocently in unison. Then they laughed and embraced.

"Let's do this," said Kim's mom.

"And I will stay here and watch the twins," Kim's dad said from the living room. "And maybe order a pizza," he mused.

"Oh! What toppings?" asked Ron. Then he realized Kim and her mom and nana had already run out the door. "Oh, right! Mission mode!" he said.

Rufus popped out of Ron's backpack and pointed to the drone. chittering with an idea.

Drakken woke from a nap, covered in empty milk cartons. "Time to bring this evil plan home," he murmured to himself. He sat up and said, "Fire up the brain modulator." He noticed his machine was missing and instantly bolted to his feet. "Where is my machine?" he asked the empty room. "The brain modulator! Shego! Shego!"

There was a grating sound, and the wall to the grimy lab opened. Drakken entered a high-tech laboratory off from the main lair, then watched from on high as Shego and Athena input stats into a huge, evil-looking machine.

Drakken was completely stunned. He looked around the room. It was the lair of his dreams! Shiny, chrome, and completely packed with evil stuff, including his brain modulator machine!

"Wait, quick question: was this here the entire time?" asked Drakken.

"Oh yeah, I guess with everything going on it just slipped my mind," Shego said with a smirk.

Drakken was annoyed. But he couldn't stay mad for long; this new lair was so fantastic! He took out his phone and snapped a picture while Athena continued fiddling with knobs and switches on Drakken's giant machine.

"I gotta post this to Villain-stagram! They'll have epic FOMO!" he said as he took a selfie.

Shego interrupted him. "Hey! Make with the evil plan."

Drakken reached into a deep pocket and pulled out the glowing blue cube. He walked over to the machine, inserted the cube, and closed a panel as Athena and Shego looked on. The machine lit up, filling the lair with a creepy blue light. It started to make a humming noise. Two panels on the machine slid open, each revealing a chamber large enough to hold a person.

"Yes! Yes! Yes!" cheered Drakken.

"So, about my next mission . . ." Athena said, unimpressed.

"Dear, tiny, purple Athena, you'll get your next mission, guaranteed," said Drakken.

Shego noticed Athena's look of uncertainty. "Okay! Let's go get you ready for your big, fun surprise," she said, leading Athena away.

Meanwhile, on the roof of the lair, Kim was trying to figure out how to get inside.

"Hey, Wade? Are you sure this is it?" she asked, looking at a skylight coming out of the grassy ground.

"Definitely. The energy readings are off the charts," he responded.

Kim tapped her Kimmunicator. She needed backup. "Come in, Team Golden Girls," she said.

"Very funny. You're grounded," said Kim's mom.

"I'm gonna sneak in through the skylight and find Athena. Is the alarm neutralized?" Kim asked.

Down below, Kim's mom and nana were standing in front of an elaborate fuse box. Nana gave the box a roundhouse kick, sending sparks flying everywhere.

"Is now," answered Nana.

"Thanks, Nana. You guys rendezvous with Ron. I'm going in," she said. She used her laser lip balm to cut a hole through the glass of the skylight, then jumped through the hole. She landed silently, peeking into the lair from behind a door.

Kim saw Shego standing over Athena in a dark room lit only by a vanity. Athena was sitting in front of the vanity mirror. Shego walked away, leaving Athena alone.

This was Kim's chance! She ran up to Athena.

"Athena! We're here! Come on, let's go!" Kim said.

Athena turned to Kim. She looked disgusted.

"I'm not going anywhere with you, Kim," Athena said with contempt.

"You're mad. I get that. I'm sorry. I really messed up at the assembly, I know," said Kim.

"Kim," said Athena, turning in her chair to look Kim in the face, "you were a garbage friend way before the fight at the assembly!" Athena stared harder at her. "It was great when I was your pet project who blew up your ego. *You're the best, Kim! I can't believe I'm doing a friendship with Kim Possible!*" Athena mocked. "But the moment that I started to surpass you, you fell apart."

"You're right," said Kim. "I was so caught up in all my drama, but I'm better now, thanks to you," she said with utmost sincerity.

Athena shrugged dramatically. "You're sorry. And you're better now! I'm so happy for you!" said Athena sarcastically. "But my purpose here was not to be your friend who inspires you."

Just then, Athena's face opened up, revealing a

creepy robot mechanism within. Kim was completely stunned. Athena was a robot! "As you can see, I'm far more complex than that," Athena added.

"What?" said Kim, who was struggling to come to terms with the fact that her friend was a robot.

"My purpose was to *destroy* you." Athena's face snapped shut. "And I nailed it. And now Drakken and Shego have a new mission for me, and whatever it is, I know it's gonna be great."

"Athena, you can't trust them!" pleaded Kim, trembling. "I know there's still good in you."

Athena moved past Kim and headed for the door.

Kim spun to face her. "Athena!"

"Kim, just stop. You should get out of here while you still can," Athena said from the doorway.

"Don't leave!" Kim called out.

But it was too late. Athena was gone.

Kim paced around the lair and noticed all the moments of their brief friendship scattered around the room. Photos of Kim and Ron. Newspaper clippings. Mementos from Bueno Nacho, the hair salon, and more. Kim felt a heaving in her chest as she realized that all this time, Athena had been tricking her. Athena had never wanted to be Kim's best friend. She had wanted to *be* Kim. Or had they truly been friends?

Shego and Drakken were strapping Athena into one of the chambers in the machine. They tightened the restraints around her, then placed a skullcap covered in wires on her head.

"Comfy?" asked Drakken.

"I guess! Why do I need these?" Athena asked, looking down at her restraints with an innocent smile.

"A safety precaution. Mostly ours," answered Shego. The doors to the chamber holding Athena closed, and Drakken and Shego shared an evil cackle.

Just then, the door to the lab slide open. Kim, her mom and nana, and Ron flew into formation.

"Hey, Drak!" called out Kim.

"Possible!" shouted Drakken.

"You're kidding!" said Shego.

"Mind if we crash the party?" asked Kim.

"Oh, I was counting on it," replied Drakken as he

clicked a remote control. Suddenly, a giant column of light from the ceiling surrounded them! It was a force field! There was no escape!

"Hey!" shouted Ron. He glanced down and saw that the lasers from the force field had cut through Ron's backpack, and it—along with the drone inside—had fallen outside of the force field. Rufus peeked out of the bag. "Rufus!" Ron cried.

Kim, Ron, Kim's mom, and Nana stayed clear from the laser beams of the pillar that held them.

"Nice, right?" Drakken called out.

"It's okay, buddy! We'll be out of here soon," Ron said to Rufus, who scurried around on the floor, scared.

"This lair has it all. And that force field is one hundred percent inescapable, because the off switch is *all the way up there*!" He pointed to a gigantic red OFF switch on the ceiling.

"Don't tell them where it is," said Shego, shaking her head.

"Shego!" Drakken snapped back.

"Kim!" came Wade's voice. "I can't hack this force field."

"Anywho, welcome to my long-awaited victory," Drakken continued. "As I rotted away in that cell . . ."

"Ugh! The evil plan reveal," Nana said with an eye roll.

"I should have brought a book," said Kim's mom.

"I find these informative. They fill in some of the blanks," added Ron.

"Do you mind? Where was I?" Drakken asked.

"Rotting in your cell," answered Ron.

"Yes, yes, yes! It was there that I realized that you, Kim Possible, had something special. Something that separated you from everyone else," Drakken explained. "So, I created a cybertronic humanoid."

Shego gestured to Athena, who stood in the glass chamber hooked up to the wires.

"What?" came Wade's voice. "Athena's a *robot*?"

"I sent her in to befriend you. To learn from you," Drakken continued. "And to steal what makes you . . . Possible, creating a digital version of your . . . *spark*."

Kim looked at Athena. "My spark?" she said.

"Your spark," Drakken repeated.

"Kimitation," Kim murmured in realization.

"You should trademark that," said Drakken.

"Or Kim-puter. Kim-puter is good, too," added Shego.

"And now I am going to transfer that digital spark from her to *me*!" Drakken said, pointing from Athena to an empty chamber on the other side of the machine. "Because you plus me equals invincible!"

So this was Drakken's evil master plan.

"It should also make me bigger and stronger!" Drakken added.

Kim couldn't believe it. What was she going to do now?

"Wait, what happens to Athena?" Kim's mom asked.

"Oh, well. She'll be destroyed," answered Drakken matter-of-factly.

"What? *No!*" shouted Kim, stepping forward but getting zapped by the laser bars. She backed away.

"You gotta break a few eggs, kid," said Shego.

Athena was clearly scared. She struggled against her restraints. Kim was trapped in the beam of light, unable to help her friend.

"I'm gonna get you out of there, Athena!" Kim said.

"Why? She's just a robot," said Drakken.

"You're wrong. She's my friend," said Kim firmly.

"That's actually quite touching. Now, let's see how close of a family you can become," Drakken said as he pulled a lever down. The force field around Ron, Kim, Kim's mom, and Nana started shrinking! There was no way out!

"Stay away from the sides!" Nana called out.

"Careful, everyone!" said Kim's mom.

Wade's voice sounded. "Guys, that thing's going to vaporize you! I can't stop it!" he cried.

Just then, Rufus saw his friends in danger. He looked at the button on the wall, gathered up his courage, and leapt onto the drone.

"Oh! Good call, Rufus! I'm on it!" Wade powered up the drone and flew it into the air with Rufus aboard. Rufus uttered a fierce battle cry.

"That's my boy! He's Ru-fast and Ru-furious!" said Ron proudly.

The drone flew toward the ceiling and the OFF switch! But before Rufus could get there, Shego saw what he was up to. She started shooting fiery plasma rays right at the drone. She landed a direct hit!

"Rufus!" Ron shouted.

Rufus jumped off the drone right as it exploded. He hit the OFF switch, freeing his friends! The zapping force field around them vanished. Then Rufus fell toward the ground, landing perfectly in Ron's hands.

"Get yourself a mole rat who saves the day! Also, naked!" said Ron.

Kim didn't waste a second. She lunged toward Shego.

Mom and Nana cornered Drakken to keep him from escaping. He was cowering in the corner.

"You know, we really need to do this more often," said Nana.

"Yeah!" said Kim's mom, pushing Drakken as Nana knocked him to the floor.

Kim kicked Shego away.

Across the lair, Drakken pushed a button. Smoke sprayed out at Kim's mom and nana, and then a net fell from the ceiling and trapped them.

Drakken ran toward his chamber in the machine.

"Kim!" Ron shouted, pointing.

Drakken put the skullcap on and shouted, "Shego! The switch!"

Shego reached out an arm and sent a blast at the switch! The machine roared to life and glowed blue. Energy flowed from Athena to Drakken through sparking tubes connecting one chamber to the other. The blue light surrounded Athena and Drakken.

"Youth! Vitality! Killer moves! Mad skills! *Spark!*" he yelled as the blue energy around him grew brighter. His whole body sparked and glowed.

Athena looked terrified. "Help!" she called with a weakened voice.

"Kim! The brain modulator! If you can disrupt it—" Wade said.

Kim was way ahead of him. She pushed forward, whipped out her laser lip balm, and fired! The laser blasted across the machine and hit the glowing cube. Sparks went flying!

"Noooo!" shouted Drakken while the machine continued to go haywire. The light and energy around Drakken started flowing back into Athena. "No! No!"

Kim watched as Drakken disappeared in a cloud of smoke.

When the smoke cleared, a pale blue-tinted child in an oversized outfit was standing where Drakken used to be. The child was wearing Drakken's clothes. The doors to the chamber opened and he stepped out, falling and coughing.

Kim launched into action, racing to Athena's side. Athena slumped over in her chamber. Kim couldn't figure out a way to get her out of it! Ron, Kim's mom, and Nana joined her to help.

"Shego, get them!" cried the young Drakken. "Wait, what happened to my clothes?" he asked himself. "What's wrong with my voice?"

Shego walked over, looked down at him, and burst into laughter.

"Oh, this is fan-Drakken-tastic!" Shego laughed.

"Silence, Shego!" whined the child version of Drakken.

Shego kept laughing.

Just then, the machine started to rumble and shake. Blue light began to shoot out all over the lab.

Shego stopped laughing. She looked concerned. "Uh-oh."

"It's destabilizing!" shouted the squeaky mini Drakken.

The floating cube in the machine had turned red

and begun to spit forked bolts of lightning into the room. Shego clicked something on her arm cuff.

A hatch in the floor sprang open, revealing an escape pod. Shego pushed Drakken inside. "Get in the pod, Junior."

"They're going to be blown to bits!" said Drakken. He waved behind the glass. "Bye!"

Shego rolled her eyes beside him. The pod dropped down through the floor, underground and out of sight.

Kim opened Athena's chamber door as the room shook.

"Guys!" came Wade's voice. "That thing's going to explode!" he said, referencing the glowing cube. Kim unhooked the straps around Athena, looped an arm around her, and led her out of the lair, with Ron, Kim's mom, and Nana running in the lead.

Lightning lit up the room, and Kim and Athena were blasted off their feet. Then Athena stood up and turned to the sparking machine. Athena guarded Kim from the lighting bolts, which hit Athena again and again. She stood strong, able to withstand the force.

"Athena!" Kim cried, standing. "What are you doing?"

Athena grabbed a pipe and turned to her. "Kim, go!" Athena pleaded. "You need to get out of here. I have to stay behind! I'm the only one who can do this!"

Kim took the pipe out of her hands. "No! Stop! It'll kill you!" she cried.

"I can absorb the energy, Kim! I'm not human!" Athena cried. "Only I can do this!"

Kim's mom and nana called to them from the lair door. "Come on! Run!" they shouted in unison.

"Kim, please!" Athena begged.

Kim shook her head, crying.

"Everyone will die if I go with you, Kim!"

"I'm not going to leave you here!" Kim said through tears.

"*You* saved *me*," said Athena. "Let *me* save *you*."

Kim hesitated. Then she held the pipe out to Athena.

"Go," Athena said. Then she took the pipe, launched herself into the air, and jabbed it into the cube. She was completely consumed by orange-red energy.

Kim's family pulled her away. They ran out of the lair just as it exploded behind them! The building crumbled in black smoke.

Coughing, Kim stood and turned to look at the crater of rubble. Kim's mom, Nana, and Ron stood by her side. Rufus jumped out of Ron's pocket and ran off down the hill.

"Rufus! Where are you going?" Ron called after him.

Everyone followed.

Rufus leapt from rock to rock until he found . . . Athena's hand sticking out from the rubble.

"Athena!" cried Kim, relieved. "We're gonna get you out of there!" Kim tugged on Athena's hand. She pulled it free, but it wasn't attached to anything. There were just sparking wires trailing out of the wrist. *"Aiee!"* shouted Kim. The hand twitched and then pointed a few feet away.

"Uh, Kim," said Athena. "I could use a hand." Kim gave Athena's hand to her mom and continued across the smoking debris. Kim crouched down and picked up Athena's head.

Ron joined Kim as Athena's eyes flickered and opened.

"We're going to patch you up, good as new, okay? I promise," said Kim.

"You're a really good . . . friend," said Athena.

"So are you," said Kim with a smile.

Ron rested a hand on Kim's shoulder. "She learned from the best."

Kim smiled at Ron. "So did I."

Kim heard her mom on the watch phone with her dad. "Honey, get the tiny screwdrivers out. How would you like to rebuild a cybertronic humanoid?" Kim's mom said with a smile.

Hi, there. Kim here again.

So things went back to normal. Or at least as normal as the life of a high school crime fighter can be. It took some time and a mega amount of coding, but we stabilized Athena, flushed out Drakken's evil programming, and saved the good in her. Which was a lot.

Together we formed a martial arts club, and it's become the hottest new thing at Middleton High. As for me, learning to be a better friend made me a better hero. And nothing can stop me now.

Character

Profiles

The International Crime Fighter

Name:	Kim Possible
Top Fashion Accessory:	Kimmunicator
Strengths:	Rescuing dudes in distress, wardrobe quick changes, navigating international tax laws, acrobatics, stopping bad guys
Known For:	Thwarting evil masterminds
Last Seen:	Saving the world

Name:	Ron Stoppable
Top Skill:	Teamwork
Strengths:	Sidekicking, knowing just what to say
Known For:	Tripping over his own shoelaces
Last Seen:	Devouring a plate of nachos at Bueno Nacho

The Best Friend Slash Sidekick

The Tech Genius

Name:	Wade Load
Top Tech:	Computer
Strengths:	All things tech, gathering intel
Known For:	His computer collection
Last Seen:	As a hologram talking with Kim

Name:	Rufus Stoppable
Top Trait:	Courage
Strength:	Friendship
Known For:	Being cute
Last Seen:	In Ron's backpack

The Naked Mole Rat

The Archrival

Name:	Bonnie Rockwaller
Top Attribute:	Crushing it at soccer
Strengths:	Imparting her sophomore-sister wisdom to the new freshmen
Last Seen:	Practicing soccer drills with the team
Catchphrase:	Kthanksbye!

Name:	Athena
Top Technique:	Using her bo staff
Strengths:	Her signature move: the pole-vault spin kick, math, being a fast learner
Known For:	Liking the Cha-Cha-Chimirito (no sour cream)
Last Seen:	Hanging out with Kim

The New Girl